OCT   2011

Miss Daisy Is Crazy!

Miss Daisy Is Crazy!

Dan Gutman

Pictures by
Jim Paillot

HarperTrophy®
An Imprint of HarperCollinsPublishers

Harper Trophy® is a registered trademark of
HarperCollins Publishers Inc.

Miss Daisy Is Crazy!
Text copyright © 2004 by Dan Gutman
Illustrations copyright © 2004 by Jim Paillot

Library of Congress Cataloging-in-Publication Data
Gutman, Dan.
    Miss Daisy is crazy! / Dan Gutman ; pictures by Jim Paillot.— 1st ed.
      p.   cm. — (My weird school ; #1)
    Summary: Miss Daisy's unusual teaching methods surprise the second grade
students, especially reluctant learner A.J.
    ISBN 0-06-050700-4 (pbk.) — ISBN 0-06-050701-2 (lib. bdg.)
    [1. Schools—Fiction. 2. Teachers—Fiction. 3. Learning—Fiction.
4. Humorous Stories.] I. Paillot, Jim, ill. II. Title.
PZ7. G9846Mk 2004   2003021441
[Fic.]—dc22   CIP
                                                                          AC

Typography by Nicole de las Heras
❖
First Harper Trophy edition, 2004
Visit us on the World Wide Web!
www.harperchildrens.com

10 11 12 13 LP/CW 40 39 38 37 36 35 34 33 32

To Emma

Contents

I Hate School!

"My name is A.J. I like football and video games, and I hate school." Our teacher, Miss Daisy, was taking attendance. It was the first day of second grade. Miss Daisy told everyone in the class to stand up, say our name, and say something about ourself.

All the kids laughed when I said I hated school. But there was nothing funny about it. I have learned a lot in my eight years. One thing I learned is that there is no reason why kids should have to go to school.

If you ask me, kids can learn all we need to learn by watching TV. You can learn important information like which breakfast cereal tastes best and what toys you should buy and which shampoo leaves your hair the shiniest. This is stuff that we'll need to know when we grow up.

School is just this dumb thing that grown-ups thought up so they wouldn't have to pay for baby-sitters. When I grow up and have children of my own, I won't make them go to school. They can just ride their bikes and play football and video games all day. They'll be happy, and they'll think I'm the greatest father in the world.

But for now, I wanted to let my new teacher, Miss Daisy, know from the very start how I felt about school.

"You know what, A.J.?" Miss Daisy said, "I hate school too."

"You do?"

We all stared at Miss Daisy. I thought teachers loved school. If they didn't love school, why did they become teachers?

Why would they ever want to go to a school as a grown-up? I know that when I'm a grown-up, I'm not going to go anywhere near a school.

"Sure I hate school," Miss Daisy continued. "If I didn't have to be here teaching you, I could be home sitting on my comfortable couch, watching TV and eating bonbons."

"Wow!" we all said.

"What's a bonbon?" asked Ryan, a kid with black sneakers who was sitting next to me.

"Bonbons are these wonderful chocolate treats," Miss Daisy told us. "They're about the size of a large acorn, and you can pop the whole thing right in your mouth so you don't need a napkin. I could eat a whole box of bonbons in one sitting."

"They sound delicious!" said Andrea Young, a girl with curly brown hair. She was sitting up real straight in the front of the class with her hands folded like they were attached to each other.

Miss Daisy seemed like a pretty cool lady, for a teacher. Anybody who hated school and liked to sit around watching TV and eating chocolate treats was okay by me.

Me and Miss Daisy had a lot in common. Maybe going to school wouldn't be so terrible after all.

2

Dumb Miss Daisy and Principal Klutz

Miss Daisy said it was time for us to clear off our desks and see how much we knew about arithmetic.

Ugh!

"If I gave you fifty-eight apples and Principal Klutz took twenty-eight of them away," Miss Daisy asked, "how many apples would you have left? A.J.?"

"Who cares how many apples you would have left?" I said. "I hate apples. If you ask me, you and Principal Klutz can take all the apples away and it wouldn't bother me one bit."

"You would have thirty apples," said that girl Andrea Young in the front of the class. She had a big smile on her face, like she had just opened all her birthday presents. Andrea Young thinks she's so smart.

"I hate arithmetic," I announced.

"You know what?" Miss Daisy said. "I hate arithmetic too!"

"You do?" we all said.

"Sure! I don't even know

8

what you get if
you multiply four
times four."

"You don't?"

"I have no idea,"
Miss Daisy said, scratch-
ing her head and wrinkling up her forehead like she was trying to figure it out.
"Maybe one of you kids can explain it to
me?"

Boy, Miss Daisy was really dumb! Even I know what you get when you multiply four times four. But that smarty-pants-I-know-everything-girl Andrea Young beat me to it and got called on first.

"If you put four crayons in a row," she told Miss Daisy as she put a bunch of crayons on the top of her desk, "and you make four rows of four crayons, you'll have sixteen crayons. See?" Then she counted the crayons from one to sixteen.

Miss Daisy looked at the crayons on Andrea's desk. She

had a puzzled look on her face.

"I'm not sure I understand," she said. "Can somebody else explain it to me?"

Michael Robinson, this kid wearing a red T-shirt with a dirt bike on it, explained four times four again, using pencils. He had sixteen pencils on his desk, in four rows of four pencils. Miss Daisy still had a look on her face like she didn't understand.

"What would happen if you subtracted half of the pencils?" she asked.

Michael took away two of the rows of pencils and put them in his pencil box.

"Then you would have eight pencils!"

we all said.

Andrea Young added, "Half of sixteen is eight."

Miss Daisy wrinkled up her forehead until it was almost like an accordion. She still didn't get it!

She started counting the pencils on Michael's desk out loud and using her fingers. She got it all wrong. We gathered around Michael's desk and tried to explain to Miss Daisy how to add, subtract, multiply, and divide numbers using the pencils.

Nothing worked. Miss Daisy had to be the dumbest teacher in the history of the world! No matter how many times we tried to explain, she kept shaking her head.

"I'm sorry," she said. "It will take me a while to understand arithmetic. Maybe you can explain it to me more tomorrow. For now we have to clean off our desks because Principal Klutz is going to come in and talk to us."

I know all about principals. My friend Billy from around the corner, who was in second grade last year, told me that the principal is like the king of the school. He runs everything.

Billy says that if you break the rules, you have to go to the principal's office, which is in a dungeon down in the basement. Kids in the dungeon get locked up and are forced to listen to their parents' old CDs for hours. It must be horrible.

Miss Daisy told us to be on our best behavior so Principal Klutz would see how mature we were. Finally he walked into our room.

"Welcome to the second grade," he said cheerfully. "I'm sure we are all going to have a wonderful year together."

Principal Klutz said a lot of stuff about the rules of the school. We're not allowed to run in the halls, and we're not allowed to chew gum. Stuff like that.

But I wasn't listening very closely

because I kept staring at his head. He had no hair at all! I mean none! His head looked like a giant egg.

When Principal Klutz was all done telling us the rules of the school, he asked if anybody had any questions about what he had said.

"Did all your hair fall out of your head," I asked, "or did you cut it off?" Everybody laughed, even though I didn't say anything funny. Miss Daisy looked at me with a mean face.

"Actually, it was both," Principal Klutz

replied with a chuckle. "Almost all of my hair fell out on its own, so I decided to shave the rest of it off."

"That's the saddest story I ever heard!" said this girl named Emily, and she burst into tears.

"Don't feel bad," Principal Klutz said. "It could have been a lot worse."

"How?" sniffled Emily.

"Well, at least my brain didn't fall out of my head!"

We all laughed, even Emily. Principal Klutz was a pretty funny guy, for a principal.

"Any other questions?"

"Do you have a dungeon down in the

basement where you put the bad kids?" I asked.

"Actually, the dungeon is on the third floor," Principal Klutz replied.

Nobody laughed this time. He quickly told us that he was just making a joke and that he didn't even have a dungeon at all.

Principal Klutz must have felt bad that we didn't think his joke was funny, because he invited us all up to the front of the room to touch his bald head.

We did, and that made everybody feel a lot better.

Principal Klutz seemed nice, but a lot of people seem nice when you first

meet them. Then later you find out that
they are evil villains who plan to take

over the world.

I bet he was lying about the dungeon.

How to Spell Read

Before school started, my mother told me that second grade was the most interesting grade because this was the year that I would be able to read chapter books all by myself. I already knew how to read, even though I had tried very hard not to learn.

You see, my friend Billy told me that you really don't have to know how to read. Billy says that when you grow up and make lots of money, you can pay people to read for you. That sounded good to me.

"I hate reading," I announced when Miss Daisy passed out some spelling worksheets.

"Me too!" agreed Miss Daisy.

"You do?" we all asked.

"Yup," she said. "I can't read a word."

"You can't?"

"Nope."

"You can't even spell the word *read*?" Michael Robinson asked.

"I don't have a clue," she said, scratching her head the same way she did when she told us she didn't know how to multiply four times four.

"Just sound it out, Miss Daisy!" Andrea suggested.

"*R-e-e-d?*" Miss Daisy said.

"No!" we all shouted.

"I give up," she said. "Do any of you know how to spell the word *read*?"

"*R-e-a-d*," we all chanted.

"Wow! I didn't know that!" marveled Miss Daisy. "You have taught me a lot today."

"How did you get to teach second grade if you don't even know how to spell *read*?" asked Ryan.

"Well, I figured that second graders don't know how to spell very well, so it wouldn't matter whether or not I could spell."

"I know how to spell lots of hard words," Andrea Young announced.

"Me too," everybody else said.

"Really?" Miss Daisy said. "Like what?"

Everybody started shouting out words and how to spell them, but Miss Daisy stopped us and made us take turns. She had each of us go up to the chalkboard and write three words we knew.

I wrote *tonight*, *writing*, and *McDonald's*.

By the time we were done, the whole chalkboard was filled with words. There wasn't even any room left for more.

"Wow!" Miss Daisy said. "You kids have taught me so much this morning. I'm really glad I decided to become a teacher."

Miss Daisy Is Crazy!

In the lunchroom I opened my lunchbox and saw that my mom had packed me a peanut butter and jelly sandwich. I traded it with Michael Robinson for his potato chips. Everybody was talking about Miss Daisy.

"Miss Daisy is crazy," Ryan said.

"She's the weirdest teacher I ever had," said Emily. "She can't read, she can't write, and she can't even do arithmetic.

What kind of a teacher is that?"

"A bad one," I said.

"Hey, I just thought of something," Michael Robinson was able to say even though his mouth was filled with peanut

butter. "Do you think that maybe Miss Daisy isn't really a teacher at all?"

"What do you mean?" Ryan asked.

"Maybe she's an impostor," said Andrea.

"An impostor? What's that?" I asked. "Somebody who imposts?"

"No, silly. An impostor is somebody who pretends to be somebody else," Andrea explained. "She might be a fake teacher."

"Maybe Miss Daisy is really a jewel thief or a bank robber," I guessed. "Maybe she snuck into the school and is hiding so the police won't catch her."

"I think *you're* the one who's crazy." Andrea giggled, choking on her milk.

But what if Miss Daisy *was* a bank robber? Or she could be a horse thief or a cattle rustler or somebody who parks where there is a yellow line on the curb. My head was starting to fill with all kinds of awful things Miss Daisy could be.

"Maybe Miss Daisy kidnapped our real teacher and is holding her for ransom!" I suggested.

"Wow, you think so?" Emily asked, looking all scared.

"What's ransom?" asked Ryan.

"My mom tells me I'm handsome," Michael Robinson claimed.

"Not *handsome*! *Ransom*!" said Andrea. "I don't know what it is, but whenever somebody is kidnapped, they get held for it."

"In cartoons people who get kidnapped are always tied up to railroad tracks," I reminded everybody. "Maybe our real teacher is tied up to some railroad tracks right now!"

"We've got to save her!" said Emily, and she went running out of the lunchroom.

"Wait a minute," said Michael Robinson. "That doesn't make sense. If Miss Daisy can't even read or do arithmetic, how is

Hee-Hee

she going to be able to kidnap a teacher and tie her to railroad tracks?"

"She doesn't look like a kidnapper to me," Ryan said.

"We should tell Principal Klutz," said Andrea. "He'll know what to do."

"No!" I shouted. "Don't you see how good we have it? If we tell Principal Klutz how dumb Miss Daisy is, he will fire her and replace her with a real teacher. A real teacher who knows reading and writing and arithmetic. We'll have to learn all that stuff. You don't want that, do you?"

"No way!" said Michael Robinson.

"I don't care if she is an impostor or a bank robber or a kidnapper," I said. "I like her. I say we keep her."

"Me too," Michael Robinson agreed. "I think she's cool."

"Okay, let's not tell anybody," I said. "It will be our little secret."

We all agreed. Our lips would be sealed. But not sealed with glue or anything. That would be gross.

The Most Genius Idea!

After lunch we had recess, which means we get to go out in the playground and run around. Miss Daisy said we needed to burn off energy.

"Now this is more my style," I announced when we got outside. I made a beeline for the monkey bars. Then

me and some other kids hit the swings. After that all the boys had a contest to see who could spin around in circles the longest without throwing up. Michael Robinson won. Then we all sat down on the grass.

Even though Miss Daisy was pretty cool, we all agreed that we hated school. We made a promise to one another that we would hate school forever, even if we changed our minds and decided that we liked school.

That's when Ryan came up with the most genius idea in the history of the world.

This was his idea: We should buy the school.

Ryan told us that his father worked for this big company and that once his father's company bought some other company just like you would go into a store and buy a candy bar. Ryan said it happens all the time. He said he didn't see any reason why we couldn't buy the school just like that.

"If we bought the school, what would we do with it?" Michael Robinson asked.

"We could do anything we want with it. We'd own it."

"Could we turn it into a video-game

arcade?" I asked.

"Sure, why not? Instead of teaching reading and writing and arithmetic, we could teach kids how to play video games."

"And we could ride skateboards in the hallways?" asked Michael Robinson.

"Sure we could," Ryan said, "if we owned it."

I got all excited, because if there's one thing that I like to do almost as much as playing football, it's playing video games.

Oh, and riding skateboards. I started emptying out my pockets. I had a nickel, three pennies, and a LifeSaver. The other boys emptied their pockets too. We separated all the pennies, nickels, and dimes into little piles. Then we added up all the money. We had one dollar and thirty-two cents.

"Wow!" Michael Robinson said. "That's a lot of money!"

"I don't think it's enough to buy a school," said Ryan, who knew a thing or two about financial matters because his father worked for this big company.

"Well, how much do you need to buy a school?" I asked.

"Beats me," said Ryan. "We'd better ask Miss Daisy."

We all rushed inside after recess and asked Miss Daisy how much it would cost to buy the school.

"Gee, I don't know," said Miss Daisy, who didn't seem to know much of anything. "Why do you want to buy the school?"

"We want to turn it into a video-game arcade," I told her.

"What a great idea!" She beamed. "I love video games. There are so many schools and so few video-game arcades. It makes perfect sense to turn some of those schools into video-game arcades. I'll arrange a meeting with Mr. Klutz tomorrow so we can ask him if we can buy the school. But right now, we have to go to Mrs. Cooney's office."

Mrs. Cooney's office is down the hall from our class. She says she's the school nurse, but personally I think she's a spy. I'll tell you why. There's this big poster on her wall that says this:

I tried to read it, and it didn't make any sense at all. Even Andrea Young didn't know how to read the poster, and she knows everything. I think Mrs. Cooney has created a secret code, and she's using the poster to send mystery spy messages. I will have to keep an eye on her.

When we walked into Mrs. Cooney's office, she had us all line up in size order. I was one of the shortest kids, so I had to stand in the front of the line. Then Mrs. Cooney told us to take off our shoes. At first I thought she didn't want us to track mud all over her office. But then she told us that she was going to weigh and meas-ure us. Obviously she is trying to gather information about us, because that is what spies do.

My friend Billy says that the heavier you are, the smarter you are, because heavy people have bigger brains. But I think Billy just says that because he is overweight. I weighed fifty-two pounds.

Mrs. Cooney showed us this awesome ruler she has. It is made of metal and stretches out six feet long. When she presses a button, the whole thing shoots into her hand and disappears like magic. That is cool! I'll bet she has lots of other spy tools too.

She wouldn't let us play with her magic ruler, but Mrs. Cooney ran around measuring everything. She showed us that the bench we were sitting on was seventeen inches high. The door to her office was thirty inches across. And her foot was twelve inches long.

"Hey, my foot is a foot!" Mrs. Cooney exclaimed.

"Aren't all feet feet?" I asked.

"Some feet are less than a foot, and some feet are more than a foot," she replied. "But my foot is exactly a foot."

I had no idea what she was talking about.

Mrs. Cooney

wrapped the meas-
uring tape around
her forehead and
announced, "Look!
My head is almost
two feet in circumference!"

I knew that circumference was the distance all the way around a circle and
diameter was the distance through the
middle of a circle.

"What's the diameter of your head, Mrs.

Cooney?" I asked. Everybody laughed, even though I didn't say anything funny.

"That would be hard to measure. But isn't measuring things fun?" Mrs. Cooney asked. "I wonder how much the scale weighs."

Mrs. Cooney started to measure and weigh more things, but Miss Daisy said we had to go back to class.

What Do You Want to Be?

At the end of the day, Miss Daisy sat on the floor and we all sat around her. She told us to talk about what we want to be when we grow up.

"I want to be a veterinarian," said Andrea Young.

"Does anyone know what the word

veterinarian means?" asked Miss Daisy.

"That's somebody who doesn't eat meat," said Michael Robinson.

"It is not!" I said. "That's a vegetarian. A veterinarian is somebody who fought in a war."

"That's a veteran," Miss Daisy said. "Andrea, would you like to tell the class what a veterinarian does?"

"A veterinarian is an animal doctor."

That Andrea Young thinks she knows everything. But for once, I knew she was wrong.

"Animals can't be doctors," I said.

Everybody laughed, even though I didn't say anything funny. Miss Daisy said a veterinarian is a doctor who takes care of animals. That made a lot more sense than that dumb thing Andrea said.

Emily was next and she said she wanted to grow up and become a nurse in a hospital.

"Why do you want to do that?" I asked. "People come into hospitals all sick and injured, their arms falling off, their guts hanging out. . . ."

"A.J.!" Miss Daisy said in her serious voice.

Emily got all upset and ran out of the room crying.

"What did I say?" I asked.

"What do you want to be when you grow up, A.J.?" Miss Daisy asked.

"I'm going to be a famous football

47

player," I said.

"Really? And why did you choose that field?"

"Because I love football," I said, "and if I was a football player, I wouldn't have to read or write or do arithmetic or go to school. My friend Billy told me that foot-

ball players are really dumb."

"Your friend told you that?" said Miss Daisy.

"Yeah, Billy is really smart. He also told me that if you dig a hole deep enough, you can dig all the way to China. And if you fall into that hole, you'd fall all the way through the Earth and pop right out the other side. And you'd be moving so fast that you'd shoot all the way into outer space."

Michael Robinson said that sounded cool. He decided that instead of becoming a firefighter, he wanted to become one of those hole-digging astronauts.

Emily came back into the room with

a tissue. Everybody else went around in a circle saying what they wanted to be. This girl named Lindsay said she wanted to be a singer. Ryan said he wanted to be a businessman like his dad.

Andrea Young said that if she couldn't be a veterinarian, she wanted to be a teacher like Miss Daisy. Then she gave Miss Daisy a big smile.

I hate her.

Bonbons and Footballs

The next day, Miss Daisy brought in a box with ribbons on it and told us she had a surprise.

"What's in the box?" we pleaded.

"It's a secret."

"Pleeeeeeeeeeeeeeeeeease?"

"Well, okay," she said, opening the box.

"It's bonbons!"

Miss Daisy said she thought we might be able to use them for arithmetic problems so we could learn together. She put the bonbons on the table in the front of the room. There must have been twenty or thirty of them. "Can somebody think up an arithmetic problem using bonbons?" she asked. "Andrea?"

"If you had three bonbons in a box," said Andrea as she put three bonbons into her pencil box, "and you had three boxes just like that, how many bonbons would you have all together?"

Miss Daisy looked at Andrea's pencil box for a long time, counting in her head and on her fingers. Any dummy would know that three boxes with three bonbons in each box would equal nine bonbons. Three times three is nine. But Miss Daisy didn't seem to know that. Finally she just opened up Andrea's pencil box and popped the three bonbons into her mouth.

"Who cares how many bonbons I would have?" she asked. "As long as I get to eat some of them!"

Miss Daisy really needs a lot of help with arithmetic.

After she had eaten her bonbons, Miss Daisy passed out bonbons for all of us and we had a bonbon party. Then she said that was enough arithmetic for the day and asked what we wanted to talk about for the rest of our math time. "Football!" I shouted.

Miss Daisy didn't like that I talked without raising my hand first. Personally, I don't see what raising my hand has to do with talking. I don't talk with my hands.

But she did let me talk, and I told her that football is just about my favoritest thing in the world and I know all about it. My dad takes me to every game of the Chargers, a professional football team.

"Maybe you can help me," Miss Daisy said. "I always wondered how long is a football field?"

"A hundred yards," I told her. "Anybody knows that."

"Wow! That's a big field. With a field that big, how can you and your father see what's going on?"

"My dad always tries to get us seats near the fifty-yard line," I said. "They're the best tickets."

"Why?" Miss Daisy asked.

"Because the fifty-yard line is right in the middle of the field."

"Does that mean that half of a hundred yards would be fifty yards?" she asked.

"Yup."

"I see," Miss Daisy said. "So if you know there are a hundred yards on a football field, do you know how many pennies there are in a dollar? Andrea?"

"A hundred!" hollered Andrea Young. "Just like a football field!"

"Really?" said Miss Daisy. "So if half the football field is fifty yards, how many pennies are in half a dollar?"

"Fifty!" Michael Robinson shouted.

"Because fifty is half of a hundred and fifty plus fifty makes a hundred!"

"And half of fifty must be twenty-five because two quarters is fifty cents!" added Emily.

"And four quarters makes a dollar!" Ryan exclaimed.

"And four quarters makes a football game, too!" Miss Daisy shouted, jumping

up and down with excitement.

"Wait a minute," I said. "I thought you told us we were finished with arithmetic."

"This wasn't arithmetic," she told us. "It was football."

"Well, okay," I said. "Just as long as you weren't trying to sneak arithmetic into our conversation about football."

"Would I do that?" Miss Daisy asked, and then she winked at me.

Sometimes it's hard to tell if Miss Daisy is serious or not.

A Lot of Books!

On Thursday Principal Klutz came into our class. He was wearing a hat, which almost made him look like a regular person who had hair on his head.

"I have to go to a meeting," Principal Klutz told us, "but I heard that some of you second graders had something important you wanted to discuss with me."

Miss Daisy said that I could ask my question.

"Can we buy the school?"

"Hmmm," Principal Klutz said. "Hmmm" is what grown-ups say instead of "er" or "um" or "uh" when they don't know what to say.

"Why do you want to buy the school?" Principal Klutz asked.

"Because we want to turn it into a video-game arcade," I told him.

"I see," the principal said. "Schools cost a lot of money."

"How much?" I asked. "If you tell us how much it will cost, we'll raise the money."

"I'll tell you what," Principal Klutz said. "I can't sell you the school, but I can rent

it to you for a night. Do you know the difference between buying and renting?"

Andrea Young got her hand up first, as usual.

"When you buy a video, you get to keep it forever," she said. "If you rent it, you have to return it to the video store in a couple of days."

"That's right," the principal said. "Would you be interested in renting the school for a night?"

"How much would that cost?" I asked.

"One million pages," Principal Klutz replied.

"Huh?"

"If you kids read a million pages in books, you can turn the school into a video-game arcade for one night."

A million pages! That sounded like a lot of books.

"How about a thousand pages?" I suggested.

"A million," said Principal Klutz. "That's my final offer. Take it or leave it."

"Would it be okay if some of the other

classes helped us out?" Miss Daisy asked.

"Certainly," Principal Klutz said. "The more the merrier. And I'll tell you what I'm going to do. If the kids in this school read a million pages, I will come to the big video-game night dressed in a gorilla suit."

"You've got a deal!" I said, rushing forward to shake Principal Klutz's hand.

In my head I was already hatching a plan.

9

Put Those Books Away

As soon as I got home from school, I went up to my big sister Amy's room.

Amy is in fifth grade, so she knows lots of things.

"You've got to help me!" I said. "If the school reads a million pages in books, Principal Klutz will put on a gorilla suit and let us turn the school into a video-game arcade!"

"I would do anything to see that," Amy said.

Amy knows how to work the computer really well. She helped me make posters that said LET'S TURN OUR SCHOOL INTO A VIDEO-GAME ARCADE! and LET'S TURN PRINCIPAL KLUTZ INTO A GORILLA!

We tacked the posters up all over Main Street. Amy sent e-mails and instant messages to all the kids in the fifth grade. The next morning we tacked the posters up all over school. I passed them out to the kids I saw. Mrs. Roopy, the school librarian, said we could put up some posters in the library. Miss Lazar, the custodian, said we could put some up in the lunchroom and the bathrooms. Mr. Loring, the music teacher, said we could put some up in the music room.

By the middle of the day, everyone in the school was reading like crazy! Kids were reading during lunch. Kids were reading during recess! Kids were plowing their way through books and then running to the school library to ask Mrs. Roopy if they could check out more. I read a book about frogs, and I don't even care anything about frogs.

Some of the teachers were starting to get mad, because kids were reading books when they were supposed to be doing other things.

"Please put those books away," Miss Daisy had to tell us. "It's time for reading."

Miss Daisy said she was sorry that she wouldn't be able to help us very much because she didn't know how to read. But she was nice enough to draw a big mural in the hallway with a giant thermometer on it. Every time we read a lot of pages, she would make the temperature line on the thermometer go up. At the top of the thermometer were the words *One million.*

Soon kids were bursting into our room and yelling, "Mrs. Biggs's class has read another five hundred pages!" and "Miss

Hasenfratz says to add another six hundred pages!" It was fun watching the temperature go up.

At the end of a week, our school had read almost a half a million pages!

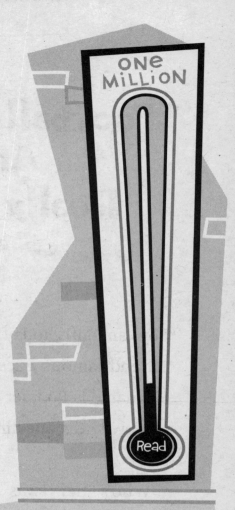

10

Football Players Are Really Dumb

"Boys and girls, today we have a very special and famous guest," Miss Daisy said. "His name is Boomer Wiggins."

"Wow!" was the first thing everybody said.

"Who's he?" was the second thing everybody said.

But I knew who Boomer Wiggins was. Because Boomer Wiggins was my hero. He was the quarterback of my favorite football team, the Chargers! Wow! A real football player right in our classroom! Miss Daisy told us that Boomer Wiggins had a daughter in fourth grade, and that's why he was spending the day at our school.

When Boomer Wiggins walked into the class, everybody gasped. He was really big and had so many muscles that they poked right against his shirt! We all crowded around him, and Boomer let us feel his arm muscles. I couldn't even get my hands around them! Then Boomer picked up Emily with one hand!

He was amazing. Then
he gave each of us
a little plastic
football, and he
signed his name
on each one.

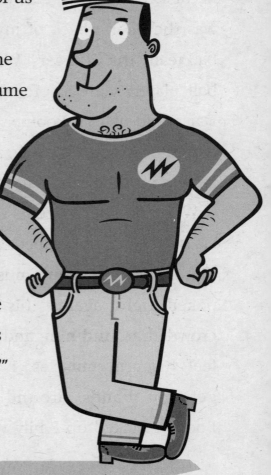

"Does
anybody
have any
questions?"
Boomer asked.

"Do you like
knocking guys
on their butts?"
I asked.

Everybody
laughed,

even though I didn't say anything that was funny. Miss Daisy said it was "butt," not "butts," because a person only has one butt. But I said a butt was divided into two halves, so really it could be "butts." Miss Daisy said that was enough of that talk. I said she shouldn't be complaining because she was the one who started it.

"I don't like knocking people down," Boomer told us, "but sometimes we have to because it's part of the game."

"Mr. Wiggins," asked Miss Daisy, "is it true that football players are really dumb?"

We all gasped. I was afraid Boomer Wiggins might knock Miss Daisy on her butt.

"Excuse me?" Boomer said, like he wasn't sure if he had heard the question.

"Well, somebody once told me that if you play football, you don't have to know how to read or write or do arithmetic or go to school."

"Who told you that?" Boomer asked Miss Daisy.

Everybody looked at me. I slid down so that my head was almost under my desk, and I hid behind my notebook.

"Oh, a good friend of mine told me," Miss Daisy said. "Is it true?"

"If I didn't go to school, I never could have become a football player," Boomer told us. "I have to read and study my playbook very carefully. I have to write letters to my fans. Every week I have to study very hard to get ready for the next game."

"Did you go to college?" asked Miss Daisy.

"Yes," Boomer said, "and when my football career is over, I plan to go back to school so I can become a doctor."

"Wow!" I said. "I want to go to college someday so I can become a doctor and knock guys on their butts. I mean butt."

Everybody laughed, even though I didn't say anything funny. Then, to prove how smart he was, Boomer Wiggins read us a book and passed out bookmarks that said "Achieve Your Goal by Reading" on them.

Miss Daisy said that even though Boomer read the book to us, we could still add fifty-two pages to the total number of pages we've read.

The temperature level on the thermometer in the hallway kept getting higher and higher.

We Rule the School!

Finally the big moment arrived. It was Andrea Young (of course!) who read the one-millionth page. We all cheered when Miss Daisy went out in the hallway and filled in the top of the thermometer all the way up to the words *One million.*

That Friday night, everybody in the

whole school showed up at school. Can you believe it? I actually couldn't wait to get to school . . . on the weekend! When we got there, a big banner was hanging over the front door that said WE READ A MILLION PAGES! on it. Principal Klutz was waiting for us. He was wearing a gorilla suit, just like he promised. Inside there

was a table of snacks and treats and juice.
Miss Daisy had brought in bonbons.

But best of all, the gym was filled wall
to wall with video games!

We Read A MILLION Pages!

I had never seen so many video games in my life. Families had brought in lots of TV sets, game systems, and games, and lined them up all around the gym. We could play all we wanted, and the only rule was that you had to take turns.

For the kids who didn't like video games, there were tables of board games set up in the middle of the gym. (I think they're called board games because you get so bored playing them.)

I played just about every video game in the gym. After a few hours of staring into screens, I had a splitting headache, my hands hurt, and I thought my eyes were going to fall out of my head.

It was the greatest night of my life.

Poor Miss Daisy

Monday at school, we had social studies. Miss Daisy said she was really sorry, but she didn't know anything at all about social studies and that we would have to help her.

"I don't even know the name of the first president of the United States," she told us.

"You don't?" we all said.

"I haven't a clue."

"It was George Washington!" we all shouted.

"Really?" Miss Daisy said with a wink. "Never heard of him."

I was beginning to suspect that Miss Daisy might have been just pretending that she didn't know anything all along. One day I caught her looking at a piece of paper, and her eyes were moving back and forth like she was watching a Ping-Pong game.

"Hey, you're reading!" I said.

"I am not!" she insisted. "You know I can't read."

"Then how come your eyes are moving

back and forth like you're watching a Ping-Pong game?"

"I—I was just thinking about this great Ping-Pong game I saw once," she replied. "It was great. You should have been there."

Maybe she was joking, and maybe she wasn't. You can never tell with Crazy Miss Daisy.

If it turns out that Miss Daisy really doesn't know anything, I feel a little sorry for her. The kids in our school had read a million pages, and she couldn't read one page. The kids in our class knew how to spell, and do arithmetic and social studies. She hardly knew anything at all!

"Don't feel bad, Miss Daisy," I told her. "We'll teach you reading, writing, and arithmetic. And we won't tell Principal Klutz how dumb you are." She gave me a big hug.

It will be hard work teaching Miss Daisy everything that she doesn't know. I think that by the end of the year, if the whole class works together, we just might bring her up to second-grade level.

But it won't be easy.

Just how nuts is Mr. Klutz?

My Weird School #2
Pb 0-06-050702-0

The second book in a wacky and hilarious new series, *Mr. Klutz Is Nuts!* stars A.J., a second grader who hates school—and can't believe his crazy principal wants to climb to the top of the flagpole!

Pb: 0-06-050704-7

Don't miss *My Weird School #3: Mrs. Roopy Is Loopy*!

HarperTrophy®
An Imprint of HarperCollins*Publishers*
www.harperchildrens.com
www.dangutman.com